Marital Blitz

About the Author

Jack Ziegler, who was born in New York City, has been a cartoonist for the last fourteen years, thus not fulfilling other lifelong ambitions. His work has appeared primarily in the *New Yorker,* and also in *Esquire, National Lampoon, Psychology Today, T.V. Guide, Cosmopolitan* and *Playboy.*

Mr. Ziegler lives in Connecticut, where he is desperately trying to make his marriage happy. He (and his wife) have three children.

Also by Jack Ziegler

HAMBURGER MADNESS

FILTHY LITTLE THINGS

Marital Blitz

Jack Ziegler

 WARNER BOOKS

A Warner Communications Company

For My First Wife, Jean Ann.

Of the one hundred seventeen drawings in this collection, nineteen originally appeared in *The New Yorker*, and were copyrighted © 1975, 1977, 1978, 1980, 1981, 1982, 1983, 1984, and 1985 by The New Yorker Magazine, Inc. One drawing was originally published in *Psychology Today*, and was copyrighted © 1983 by American Psychological Association. One drawing originally appeared in *Management Review*, and was copyrighted © 1983 by American Management Associations. One drawing was originally published in *TV Guide*, and was copyrighted © 1981 by Triangle Publications, Inc. One drawing was originally published by the Chicago Tribune–New York News Syndicate, and was copyrighted © 1980 by the Chicago Tribune–New York News Syndicate, Inc.

Page 7: "THAT'S AMORÉ" Copyright © 1953 by Paramount Music Corporation. Copyright renewed 1981 by Paramount Music Corporation.

Warner Books, Inc., 666 Fifth Avenue, New York, NY 10103

 A Warner Communications Company

Printed in the United States of America
First Printing: February 1987
10 9 8 7 6 5 4 3 2 1

Library of Congress Cataloging-in-Publication Data

Ziegler, Jack.
  Marital blitz.

  1. Marriage—Caricatures and cartoons.   2. American
wit and humor, Pictorial.   I. Title.
NC1429.Z47A4   1987   741.5'973   86-18976
ISBN 0-446-38076-8 (U.S.A.) (p.b.k.)
     0-446-38075-X (Canada) (p.b.k.)

CHAPTER I

Love Rears

Its Ugly Head

"The gentleman at the end of the bar would like to buy you a drink."

"When the moon hits your eye like a big pizza pie, Miss Donaldson, that's amoré."

"Exciting, isn't it, Ms. Steenhoffel? They call it eye contact."

"Here, sweetheart. These are for you. I'm sorry they're dead,
but it was a nice gesture on my part and that's all that was intended."

"Not only am I a millionaire, my dear,
I'm a very rich millionaire."

"For Pete's sake, Ma,
I know that my bed
hasn't been slept in."

"Natalie, you know that my world revolves around you constantly, except of course on Tuesdays and Wednesdays, major holidays, and every other weekend."

"Well, all right then, if you won't marry me, will you at least let me sell you some life insurance?"

"You have to realize, of course, that only the Ritz is as big as the Ritz."

"Marry me, Linda. Share in the magic."

♥

CHAPTER II

The Most Wonderful Day Of Your Life

♠

"Not bad for a ceremony steeped in meaningless symbolism."

UNPREPARED CONFETTI

"You don't think this will screw up
our relationship, do you?"

"If this marriage doesn't enhance my career, I'm going to just scream."

"So...how long do you want to stay married for?"

Love Gum

Marital Bliss

"You don't think we'd be too plaid?"

"I'm O.K. You're O.K."

"I'd like to know how you really feel about me, Elena—
I mean, of course, me vis-à-vis you."

"You'll have to understand this, Helen—by day I'm a mild-mannered reporter for a quaint metropolitan newspaper, but at night I like to watch TV."

"How do I look?"

"No!"

"I know what you're thinking. You're thinking, 'Hey, what _is_ this crap?'"

"Sorry, honey, but I got here first."

"I see that your cult is still growing."

"I don't suppose you're in the mood to take a letter, are you?"

"And this is my husband, Jerry. He's from another world."

"Living with you these past ten years, Jean Ann, I have grown in many ways."

"Oyez! Oyez! Oyez! Oyez!"

"I love you, Julie, and I think that you love me. That's why I think it would be a good idea if you kept your stupid mouth shut."

ALL-PURPOSE EXCUSE FROM THE TWILIGHT ZONE

"Bob Smight. His day. Monday, June 21st. An overview."

"For pity's sake, Myra, I'll only be in Des Moines for two days.
It's not like I'm distancing myself from you permanently."

"Sure, sure, it's the same old story.
You get to go out every night,
and I get to sit home."

"O.K. then, maybe the answer is not 'no.' Maybe the answer is 'yes.'"

CHAPTER IV

Marital Blitz

"When we get up there, you'll meet a woman who will claim to be my wife. Pay her no heed."

"When we aked you to ghostwrite the vows for George's and my wedding, Bob, I never dreamed it would lead to this."

"I must say, darling, that I find the current
arrangement totally reprehensible."

"Well, it's not meant to be a literal mustache, for God's sake!"

"Oh, by the way, sweetheart, I thought I should tell you.
I've decided to leave the mainstream and join the lunatic fringe."

"Can we forget the Riddle of the Sphinx for five seconds and just get on with the grocery shopping?"

"Are you ignoring me on purpose or are you just ignoring me?"

"Don't listen to her. She doesn't have any opinions either."

"Funtime."

"I don't have to explain myself to you!"

"Darling, please don't talk with your mouth full."

"Jessica, get off the telephone! Tommy, turn down that radio!
Somebody, let the dog out and the cat in! Hildy, that's enough time in the shower!
Madge, honey, stop weeping softly into your pillow!"

"Oh, good heavens, no.
I was talking to Emil the dog,
not to Emil my husband."

"Jenkins, today is my wife's and my twentieth wedding anniversary.
Go down to the computer and run me a series of romantic bon mots,
sentimental pap, and other off-the-cuff remarks that will tickle
her pink."

"Price is no object, young woman, when one has a wife who is as wonderful as, I'm told, mine is."

"You were right. Maybe we should have stopped at that motel back there in the Valley of the Contented Cows."

CHAPTER V

The Spat Heard 'Round The World

"Well, well, well. The bloom is finally off the rose."

"I'm not overreacting! You are!"

"I don't like squash and I won't plant it. If you want to plant some squash, fine, but I won't eat it. If you try to serve it to me in any one of its myriad disguises, I shall track you down to the far corners of the globe and destroy your mind. I don't like squash."

"For the five-hundredth time,
I don't care how dark your tan was
last year at this time!"

EMILY'S OUTRAGEOUSLY HUGE LIST OF GRIEVANCES WAS MET BY A STRING OF UNBELIEVABLY VULGAR EPITHETS FROM TOM.

"She is woman, for Pete's sake! Hear her roar!"

"Finished with your appetizer already, sir?"

"During the next commercial,
I'm going to belt you one!"

THE MANUAL ALARM

"I must say, Elizabeth,
this isn't very supportive of you."

"I came here to quietly and unobtrusively celebrate a milestone, Celeste—not to be hassled by some dumb clown."

"And furthermore, if it hadn't been for you kids, your father and I would have been divorced a long time ago."

"What is this, Mom? A balanced diet? Three squares a day?? I hate that!"

"I'm out here—watching the darkness gather."

CHAPTER VI

Cat Yummies Again

"This is my husband, Victor. He used to be inflatable."

"The truth hurts, Leo, and this is going to hurt a lot."

"I'm adding a footnote about you to my memoirs, my precious. In 25 words or less, what would you like me to say?"

"My wife! My best friend! My favorite TV program!"

"It's me—Alice! Alice Terkleman! Your wife of 22 years!
You just don't recognize me because I'm out of context."

"Quiet now, children.
Your father has an
announcement to make."

"Well, finally! I've been standing here for hours!"

"We had a dynamite marriage, and now we're having a dynamite divorce."

"Cat Yummies _again_?"

INDEX